THE PENGUIN POETS

TANGO

Daniel Halpern was born in Syracuse, New York, in 1945. He is the author of six collections of poetry, including *Life Among Others* and *Seasonal Rights,* and is editor of *Antaeus* and the Ecco Press. He has also edited *The American Poetry Anthology* and *The Art of the Tale: An International Anthology of Short Stories.* Mr. Halpern teaches in the graduate writing program of Columbia University.

TANGO

Poems by

Daniel Halpern

PENGUIN BOOKS

PENGUIN BOOKS
Published by the Penguin Group
Viking Penguin Inc., 40 West 23rd Street,
New York, New York 10010, U.S.A.
Penguin Books Ltd, 27 Wrights Lane, London W8 5TZ, England
Penguin Books Australia Ltd, Ringwood,
Victoria, Australia
Penguin Books Canada Limited, 2801 John Street,
Markham, Ontario, Canada L3R 1B4
Penguin Books (N.Z.) Ltd, 182–190 Wairau Road,
Auckland 10, New Zealand

Penguin Books Ltd, Registered Offices: Harmondsworth,
Middlesex, England

First published in the United States of America by
Viking Penguin Inc. 1987
Published in Penguin Books 1988

Grateful acknowledgment is made for permission to reprint
an excerpt from "Private Dancer," lyrics and music by
Mark Knopfler. © 1984 Strait Jacket Songs Ltd. All rights
administered by Rondor Music (London) Ltd.
Administered in the United States and Canada by
Almo Music Corp. (ASCAP).
All rights reserved. Used by permission.

Page vi constitutes an extension of this copyright page.

LIBRARY OF CONGRESS CATALOGING IN PUBLICATION DATA
Halpern, Daniel, 1945–
Tango: poems/by Daniel Halpern.
p. cm.
ISBN 0 14 058.588 5
I. Title.
PS3558.A397T3 1988
811′.54—dc19
87-20723
CIP

Printed in the United States of America by
Arcata Graphics/Halliday, West Hanover, Massachusetts
Set in Bembo

for Drue Heinz

Acknowledgments

The author would like to thank the editors of the following publications, where some of these poems first appeared:

The Bennington Review "Amaryllis"
The Black Warrior Review "3 A.M. / The Rain"
College English "Bar Escargot: A Story," "The Hobbyist"
Crosscurrents "Señor Excellent"
The Denver Quarterly "Caravaggio"
The Kentucky Review "Naming the Unborn," "House in Damariscotta"
The Missouri Review "Below Keats's Room, First Light"
The New Republic "Summer Nights"
The New Yorker "Preparations for the End of the Evening," "The Summer Rentals"
The North American Review "Child Running"
The Ontario Review "The Title"
Open Places "Dark Night," "Hotel Carlton, Tangier: The Old City," "At Dante's Tomb," "Local," "Scars"
The Paris Review "Loose"
Ploughshares "Tango"
Poetry "The Afternoon: Mid-December," "Summer Storm"
Shenandoah "An Early Death"
The Southern Review "Pound," "Nightwork"
The Tar River Review "Pastiche"
The Threepenny Review "Walking in the 15th Century"
The Worcester Review "Like Something Out of the Ordinary," "The Lesson"

"The Summer Rentals" and "Epithalamium" were reprinted in *The Morrow Anthology of Younger American Poets.*

"Señor Excellent," "To a Friend Shot on a Mexican Bus," "Summer Nights," "Walking in the 15th Century," and "The Summer Rentals" were reprinted in *New American Poetry of the 80's.*

"Words of Advice" first appeared in *A Celebration for Stanley Kunitz on His Eightieth Birthday*, Sheep Meadow Press, New York City.

"The Death of Li Po" was published as a broadside by The Two Magpie Press, Kendrick, Idaho.

"At Dante's Tomb" is for Charles Wright.
"Scars" is for Susan Halpern.
"The Title" is for David Braxton and Joyce Carol Oates.
"To a Friend Shot on a Mexican Bus" is for Don Justice.

Special thanks to Frank Bidart for his help in preparing this collection.

Contents

Part One

Part Two

Part Three

Part Four

Part Five

Part One

Visitors

At low tide, midsummer, I walked out to the mussel beds
at tide's edge. Still wet, the blue-black shells,
trussed together with hairlike bonds, waited
for the tide to move back in. I don't walk here
at low tide—it's a landscape too recently lived in
and therefore unpredictable. But I was collecting mussels

for dinner because the markets were closed
and guests from the city expected something from the sea.
I would steam the mussels in a little vermouth and toss them
with fresh basil from the back yard and a pound of pasta.
I pulled up two or three beds and placed the clenched mollusks
in the zinc pail I brought, and as it was still early,

and mild, I walked up the beach, chiding myself for not doing so
more often. A small mist like those on Guam in the war movies
of the fifties began to roll in behind the tide.
Farther on, there was a woman in a bathing suit asleep
on her towel. I continued along, walking over the sharp,
encrusted rocks of low tide for a mile, and then started back.

The air turned cool as the wind and tide pursued the evening
in an unpleasant way. When I passed, the woman
was as I'd left her nearly an hour earlier. Her head faced away
from me, back toward the line of houses,
but I guessed she was young—her hair, the shape of her body
and its posture in sleep—still there in the cooling afternoon,

the sun about to drop through the horizon.
I stopped, hoping she would hear me and turn, surprised
out of afternoon sleep, slip on her shift, and run off to her house.
I stood awhile and then spoke to her, first softly, then louder.
Then I leaned down and touched her. She was cool, almost cold,
and very smooth. She turned to me, suddenly awake and angry.

I said I lived next door . . . she hadn't moved for so long,
the temperature going down, the tide and dinner hour approaching.
She had difficulty understanding my right to this concern.
It must have been the pail of mussels that kept her from screaming.
When she looked at it I told her I was collecting for dinner,
that I wouldn't have bothered her, it was neighborly concern,

what we're accused of not acting on in moments of trouble.
She dressed, thanked me with suspicion still afloat, and moved
off the beach. In my kitchen I found a large pot to steam open
the mussels—their shells turned darker in the electrical light
and opened for good. The guests from the city arrived
and over pasta, which they cheered, we discussed the latest

felonies reported in the city papers. I wondered
what the young woman said to those who shared her dinner.
Perhaps she told them that as she slept in the afternoon sun
the man next door knelt beside her and touched her awake,
wanted to know if she was okay as he held a zinc pail
of collected mussels. After our meal, after my friends

had retired for the night with their guest towels
and fresh linen, I walked out to the water, which was set
with a single white plate, and wandered awhile down the beach.
I imagined touching that cool flesh with no response coming back,
turning her over to discover the damage all at once, startled
not out of sleep but out of the languorous, cooling afternoon.

This is the meager distance I've allowed the dying to come,
I thought, that moment after I touched her, before she turned
her girlish face to me in accusation, as I balanced beside her
with a pail of mussels, waiting for her.

TANGO

I'm your private dancer,
a dancer for money . . .

—FROM A TINA TURNER SONG

When Celina arrived the floor was on fire.
You could tell by her hips and her mouth
she was built for the tango.

Glasses of clear amber danced the tables
on the tango rhythm. You could tell
this place was built for the tango.

The room on its axis turned, and turned the dancers
around the room
hung with the haze of tango,

the haze of cigarette smoke and the smoke
of braziered meats, the smoke of bodies—
you could tell by their hips and their mouths

they were built for the tango, the smoke
from their bodies locked onto the tango beat,
the colored lights, the white and black

dancers turning on their notes, and you could tell
they were built for the tango.
When Çelina danced she danced in dance-hall heaven,

and everyone knew she was built for the tango—
you could tell by her hips and her mouth.
When she arrived the place was already on fire.

Anita Lozano sang the tangos that night and every other.
You could tell by her mouth she was built
for tango, bearing in on the lyrics, letting them go.

The couples, by this hour built for the tango,
rose up in the heat on the sweat and sweet scent of anise,
on the voice of Anita Lozano that *was* tango—

you could tell by her mouth.
You could see how their hips followed her tango soul,
her tango lyrics. Celina took the rhythm from Anita Lozano

because she was the queen of tango,
because she was built for the tango. You could tell
by her hips and her mouth she was built for the tango.

Bar Escargot: A Story

Moe served drinks in the Bar Escargot, a youthful Liberian saved by Peter, the English owner, from a cannibalistic sect of the Masons.

I would find my way there after *tapas* at the Spanish bars above the port, after the European *paseo* along the rue de Pasteur.

The Escargot was dark, empowered with the scent of West Africa, vague felony, and some piece by Beethoven from Peter's complete works on the tape deck any hour of the day.

When I arrived, Moe was often beating a dust mouse behind one of the couches of the room, and when he saw me he set down the broom, straightened a piece of colonial furniture from the previous century, put on his white waiter's coat, and served me a beer called Stork, the national bird of Morocco.

Then he brought out the chessboard, and he and I would sit down to play before the other customers arrived from their solitary dinners.

Moe didn't talk much beyond his speaking vocabulary of twenty or thirty words, but understood everything in English, French, German, and Mogrebi.

It never took him longer than five minutes to complete a game against me, although I had won tournaments in the parks of Los Angeles.

Moe had a huge Alsatian called Parrot, trained by Peter to attack the natives; the rest of us moved without harm, casually through the bar, talking to Moe and Peter without tension.

As the night wore on the regulars began to appear at their appointed hours.

They were all solitaries, cast out from one place or another, their histories never referred to or grand fictions of the present.

They were mostly beyond seventy, living in rented rooms off the boulevard, wearing loud clothes—the males in reverse makeup, the females blurring facial lines with unsteady hands.

They met at the Escargot each night and ran through their trumped-up agendas over strange mixed drinks Peter knew—as he knew each of them, their names, the hour of their arrival, the hour they would take their leave.

Among this clientele, Moe moved like a sullen predator, laughing suddenly at nothing and continuing on, preying on empty glasses.

And Parrot, kicked from one sleeping spot to another, kept an eye on the door, an eye on the ever-moving Moe.

One evening around Christmas, Moe was taken to Beni Makada, the local house of mental detention, the state hospital, after he was caught chasing one of the regulars up the rue de Fez with Peter's meat cleaver.

A few months later he returned, but the currents that had run through him like medication had turned him into something different.

He was no longer engaged by the dust that roamed the floors of the Escargot.

And he lost now at chess, which I think broke what was left of his heart.

After that, he and Parrot stayed in the kitchen and Peter cleared the tables as he served his drinks to the regulars, who diminished as the new year started out, deserting the Bar Escargot for the Ranch Bar, its upbeat chili and Country Western music.

That summer Peter died of a blood disease and the Bar Escargot was turned over to the King.

No one knew where Moe and Parrot were, they disappeared after Peter's death, although it was rumored he had returned to Liberia aboard some freighter he caught in one of the southern ports.

After I returned to the States, I heard from a friend that a spree of killings had taken place in the Dradeb, an outlying residential district, and Moe had been discovered in the area and returned to Beni Makada for life.

The Bar Escargot, Peter, Moe, and Parrot weren't anything the long-time residents of Tangier would remember, or wish to remember—a low-class bar that might have served a Greyhound station had it been in Des Moines.

But I began to wonder about Moe in Beni Makada, and years later finally went to see him—it took weeks in green and yellow offices to get a visitor's pass.

I arrived one morning in late spring when the entire compound was enclosed in fog, and the sounds that emerged from that indistinct structure were not something you wanted to take away with you.

I was led through a series of gates and courtyards, keys and locks and sullen guards who had been there too long.

In one of the inner courtyards, a low, whitewashed door opened and a middle-aged Moe sprang out on all fours.

The light blinded him, as if it had been his first in the ten years he'd been there, and he remained stationary, confused by his sudden release and the strange voices filling the courtyard.

And then he lifted one hand to his eyes and tried to bring me back from some dark corner of his life.

From the dirt of the courtyard, he looked up at me.

His head was shaved and he wore the remains of something that looked like long underwear.

He looked up at me and laughed the laugh I remembered from the Bar Escargot. I remembered the scent of Africa rising on the clinking glasses, the ever-attentive Parrot, and the last disturbing string quartets Peter had committed to tape.

And then he grabbed my leg.

Before the guards could move, he opened his mouth as if to bite me, but instead called out into the textured air of the damp courtyard, *Parrot! Parrot!*—and then the guards had him, applying to his hard body their guards' sticks, pulling his hands behind his back and pushing his forehead into the dirt of the thickening courtyard.

And when they dragged him back to his cell, or whatever lay behind that low doorway, I saw women emerge from a room in the back of the building with small metal foil–covered trays, which they pushed into the openings cut at the base of the doorways.
They placed the trays halfway through, so the hinged door rested on whatever food was being offered.
I suppose they wanted to know who was eating without having to open the door onto whatever was alive in there.
When I left, it seemed that as the locked gates clicked open for me the trays, in unison, were pulled through the shuttered openings into the waiting darkness.

Señor Excellent

I was taken there as a child,
the old Farmer's Market on Fairfax.

Spectacular displays of fruit blossomed
everywhere you looked, and men in white

behind glass made candy, their giant vats
of chocolate bubbling like the La Brea Tar Pits.

And there was always something to eat
whichever way you turned.

But the important event at Farmer's Market
was the stop in front of Señor Excellent.

He had a vocabulary limited to one shrill catcall,
a few opening bars of a song, and a number of *hello*s

varying in pitch and intensity. What I remember now
is not what Señor Excellent said, but the wisdom

and irony in the eyes of that myna bird.
We stood around whistling and clicking

and one of us would inevitably try out a few words
of endearment. Have you ever listened carefully

to what people say to talking birds
when they think they are alone? Señor Excellent

just looked at us, his expression one of agony
and disgust. I can picture him

resting on his mauled stick, calmly breathing
and watching us—picking at something

under his wing, going down for a seed, lifting
himself back up with his candy-corn beak—

and I know that his was a life not so different,
witnessing the utterances of the human race.

The Hobbyist

In late August she decided to make Thanksgiving turkeys
out of crepe paper to sell the merchants of the Valley.
I remember rolls of it around the house that fall,

browns and tans for the body, the unlikely objects she used
for the head—the beak and wattle, those deadpan eyes
that should have been balls of amber.

Every year it was something different. When I was eight
she painted old sewing boxes, calling back
into action her set of twenty-year-old oils. The box

she kept for herself, its deep green-blue, the dusky rose
flowers and their green-black leaves, three to a side,
now holds that darkness I have come through.

One spring she sold refinished tables inlaid with mosaics
I bought with her at the local hobby center. There was no end
to the colors to choose from—bright reds and yellows,

plain whites opaque and transparent, royal purple
and forest green, deep agatelike admixtures of colors
that changed as you turned them under the neon lights

of the store—and the white powder that held those blocks
of color: *grout,* the name of something
gnarled and old, more suited to the clamps

that cut the tiles. She practiced on plywood boards
before setting the tiles into the tables and fixing them
forever, everything set out by number

once the pattern emerged. I have one of the practice boards
whose tiles never found their way into a table.
She set the tiles with glue, grouted them in,

and gave the board to me for my first departure.
The colors: cobalt blue and black, dusky rose,
and her inevitable green-blue. I use it as a platter

that carries on the surface its own history
of those years when objects are what *can* remain neutral,
can attach themselves to the ongoing memory

and become part of the lasting fabric of what can be recalled.
And later on, when it becomes impossible to participate
in such simple ways, you begin a project for yourself,

to pursue what you imagine you've a gift for—talking,
moving from place to place, keeping yourself out
of harm's way. It was something domestic I received,

handed down from that early art—turkey and table,
the painted sewing box that held her mending,
the needles and thimbles, the hundred threads.

An Early Death

It is the first death that seems so open
    to revision, as if later on,
        at some ordinary hour, the dead
            will again be with us wherever we are.

It was a Catholic funeral for the boy
    who came home one day, went to sleep
        in the lasting light of early summer,
            and didn't wake up for the evening meal.

During the service I watched his mother,
    who was Spanish, as the event burned
        dimly in her, the off-red of roses
            almost dry, a small pulsing emanation,

not light exactly but something just barely
    aglow. They couldn't agree on the cause
        of death, but for me he was just gone,
            first one day and then all the others.

It occurs to me these many years later
    that the funeral provided me
        an introduction, and then the possibility
            of resuming my own life, although

I often thought I saw my friend trimming
    the ivy in front of his house on Chandler
        during the endless summer afternoons
            of the San Fernando Valley,

the silver cross he wore filmed with dirt
    kicked up by the trimmer. By autumn
        I was able to let him go.
            He no longer appeared on our street

in his white parochial-school shirts.
Sometimes, when I sat with his mother
while she prepared her survivor's meal
and we talked in a casual way

of her son, I studied the large reproduction
of Velázquez's *Surrender of Breda*
that hung on a wall near the kitchen
where we sat. I counted the horses

and soldiers as they stood in a line,
their spears held upright, catching a diminished
amber light, posing as if for Velázquez
himself, impatient to remove their armor

and return to the tables of Rioja
and heavy bread. It is the quality
of light in that painting that brings back
my friend's Spanish mother, the vermilion

smoldering like old fire behind
the horsemen, under the unilluminated
green shake of the deciduous trees
Velázquez chose to leave out of the painting.

She talked quietly about her son
as she prepared her meals. Her sorrow
was alive, unrelinquished, without
revision. She often tried to explain

how he cared for me, our friendship;
the vocabulary was hers, her meaning
embarrassing information at that age.
She allowed me to return

something of her son, although this certainly
  didn’t occur to me then, and perhaps
    not for many years.
      It is afternoon on the East Coast—

when I think of my friend
  it is she who is there, who takes his place.
    We have both lived out that early death,
      and we have this far survived the austere light

that fixes those men in *Surrender*
  of Breda, each of them waiting around
    under the protection of Velázquez’s
      invisible trees, in the little light left them.

Summer Nights

for my mother

You took me to see your friend, a youngish man
who lived encased in iron and spoke
through a machine that made his voice
sound underwater, his head propped
in such a way that I imagined it was
unattached to what there was of his body.

In the summer of 1952, I lay awake
in the hot, endless nights
with cars drifting listlessly
down Chandler Boulevard, their lights
sliding the walls of my room and moving off
into the desperately calm summer air.

On those nights I thought of your childhood,
how the doctors wrapped your poor legs
with wool and tar, your mother bathing you
through the plagued Chicago summer—
the smell of wet wool still makes you sick.

In the night, as I awaited the morning
that could find my thin body motionless and locked,
I listened with sentimental care
to my sister crying softly to herself
in dream, you and our father talking
in a muffled way in your bedroom,
the low, barely discernible static
of his transistor radio.

It was as if in those airless rooms
there was no hope of surviving the night,
that everything was endless and dark,
with sleep coming only with the lights

of cars, the final victory of their lulling
sure movement, drifting steadily awhile
on the walls of my room, and passing on.

Heavenly Ornaments

The frame of human happiness is time.
—DEREK WALCOTT

They are, so many of them, too far away now
to recall.
Outside the moon rises and slowly

the anemic globe fills with light during a cycle of nights,
blossoming full over the ragged beaches of Maine
where those friends who remain close

lie down to sleep.
Over the Pacific rim of Los Angeles
my sisters in their new lives with others

lie down to sleep.
Over the steelworks
studding the three rivers of Pittsburgh

my mother lies down to sleep.
Where I am, the tallest oak in the back yard
clutches at the rotating night-light

as it rolls through the named figures
of constellations. .
I look into the night sky,

above the pine, above the wild apple,
the larch and rock maple,
and see the determined configurations of stars

in place at their appointed hours.
And for those too far away,
or too close—we look *for* you

as we lay our tired, mortal selves to bed
with all the constellations shining. Understand,
the heavenly ornaments burn only for the living.

Part Two

The Title

for the challenger

Late afternoon light and the devotees surround
the ring—devotees, who by *gathering around* gave the ring
its name. The heat off the desert flats refuses to lessen, returns

in waves like rounds as the principals reach the ring, climb through
the ropes, and begin the dance of robes, their hands bandaged
in a clench and muted in loud leather. Then the robes are pulled
away

by men wearing silk shirts printed with their fighters' names,
like those of bowling teams, making that link momentarily with the
balled
red gloves in motion around the ring. The bodies of the fighters

glow with the patina of warm-up, their faces glisten
with Vaseline's clear makeup. Overdressed,
the ring announcer orates the stats of the nicknamed, who

remain in constant motion against the invisible avatars
of their corners, waiting for the huddle in ring center, where
they will tap gloves once in goodwill and await the opening bell.

• • •

The challenger looks older than the declared year of birth,
but it's not a question of vanity—a challenger gives away nothing
to the champion. He's about to enter the moment of ring time

he's been given after a decade of tutoring the body to respond,
small-city bouts against tough punchers with no style and a lot of pain,
the endless mileage run through city summers, the ongoing

return of the stationary bag, swinging back to present the dead
weight
of its passive body, the spinning jump rope, the intangible opponents
that haunt the sessions of shadowboxing, the weeks of restraint.

. . .

Maybe he's twenty-nine but the commentators don't believe it.
Even the retired boxing star who wears the network's blazer
looks skeptical.

The challenger moves, warming up
in his stocking of sweat, his expression puts forward
a center of concentration below the untroubled desert sky.

He moves in a way that makes the sportswriters move forward
in their reserved seats as the referee prepares himself
in the center of the ring, speaking gently to the boxers,

explaining how he wants the fight to go, how they are
to break from the clinches, to keep their punches up, the fight
clean. The cameras begin to roll behind the lights,

and the struck bell, which holds it all,
explodes off the desert, the faces
of the devotees, and the men start forward.

Scars

They are the short stories of the flesh,
can evoke the entire event
in a moment—the action, the scent
and sound—place you there a second time.

It's as if the flesh decides to hold
onto what threatens its well-being.
They become part of the map marking
the pain we've had to endure.

If only the heart were so ruthless,
willing to document what it lived
by branding even those sensitive
tissues so information might flow back.

It's easy to recall what doesn't heal,
more difficult to call back what leaves
no mark, what depends on memory
to bring forward what's been gone so long.

The heart's too gentle. It won't hold
before us what we may still need to see.

Call

The sharp, insomniac cry of a seabird
calls me from a complicated sleep.

Outside, the even slap of bay surf
on the stones of the beach below the window.

It should be possible to turn again
on the spit of sleep and reenter what's left

of the night. But I climb down a staircase
carpeted in fifties green and go through the back door

where the dead-white moon waits bloated above the summer
boats, set in the glassy glaze of the bay's brittle.

As a child the night sometimes played the riddle-of-no-waking,
and my attempt to imagine the day I wouldn't wake

kept me awake and uneasy for the duration of the night.
It seemed that in the end we just *do* wake, regardless.

On such a night I lay struggling with the car lights
passing down Chandler Boulevard when I heard a car door

slammed hard, then the hollow clacking of a woman's
heels down Chandler toward the Tierneys' house.

The car started up fast, came to a stop
again, and I heard raised voices in the cricket-timed dark,

followed by a woman screaming through her own echo. Then
no sound. When her voice returned on the wakeful nights that followed,

I sometimes tried to imagine a woman so lonely and alone
that she volunteered for the late, difficult hours,

pursued by those who torment women in the night
from cars. Sometimes I saw my sister struggling

to free herself from what I heard that night,
to reach the best citizen of our quiet neighborhood.

Sometimes the woman became the women I slept with
as I grew through a tardy adolescence, their graceful bodies

seemed to me, as they lay in my poorly furnished rented rooms,
so frail that if they called out from their own troubled sleep

I would be there to reach through the dark to hold them
above whatever opaque waters might be rising inside them.

I hear her voice on many nights I wake from sleep alone—
like this night, coming out of sleep, not knowing

where, at first, as I put the room together.
Tonight the gulls must sleep wherever they find shelter,

although one is in the air, throwing its piercing alarm
along the coast, where I stand holding what memory has brought along,

the shrill voice wounded by fear that carries now on the cries
of the unmolested feeding birds at sunrise, just rising.

Parting Words

It's a small town somewhere
away from any serious body of water.
The sky has picked up the available dust
and the sun poaches itself
on one of the horizons.
This is where you meet, a café?
Call it the Café of Four Flowers,
where they serve chilled beer
and leave you alone
with the music one of you selected
coming in. It's dark
and the lights are colored,
the right color for what you have to say.
What was it that seemed so available
driving into this town,
that vanished when you saw her white car
in front of the café,
her pale arm in its white holster
wedged out the window, waiting
because you were late again?
Always late, isn't that right?
She thinks it means something,
right? This time it means
you don't want to be here,
a town you might have come to
before the age of attachment.
The waitress is the same woman
who serves you all over the country,
only the length of her skirt
and the color of her hair change.
She'll toss your change down
and pick it up without a smile.
Who's her lover?
Who serves her the afternoon beer?

It's this kind of thinking that keeps your mind
on subjects other than leaving,
which is why destiny has brought you here:
to make it clear why you're going
and what it means.
But she's not talking.
She's doing what she's been told
is right, she's waiting
for you to say something.
You wonder what this will mean
a year from now and already you have the answer:
it won't mean anything
because she will have forgotten all about you,
your address, the number of your phone,
and the Café of Four Flowers.
She'll be with someone
who speaks even less than you
and resigned to it.
And where will you be?
You'll be right where you are today,
in some café
with your car cooling down
in the damned parking lot.
You'll be there with nothing to say,
ready to pay the bill,
hand over a little change
to the same woman,
although she'll have dyed her hair,
and fashion will have lifted her skirt a little.

LOOSE

You're loose,
sometimes good,
and lonely almost
never, not alone
long enough.
You learned to live
feinting in and moving
away, quicker
than those who took you
seriously. But
anyone's quick
who doesn't need
to stay. With your arms
out in greeting,
your feet
already on the move,
it's only itinerary
leading you on.
And here you are,
out there,
lost to those
who didn't keep up,
lost to those
still ahead.
Around the world
you've found
a little of everything
and you've given it back,
until what is left
is what you first held,
what you think that was.

Summer Storm

All day the storm's
tried squeezing out the light,
a huge mist grows,

and the wind comes up—
nothing to take the boards off
the house, but enough

to set us all on edge,
although these winds,
unlike the easterly winds

of the Mediterranean,
carry nothing but air.
Only a few gulls

climb the wind and swing
over the house—
the diving birds gone,

the herons that feed
at the water's edge gone,
and the ducks are sheltering

somewhere out of the storm.
I have the fire started,
a little broth on the stove,

and the house is closed
to the storm—
only its light

can reach us.
It picks out the white boats
in the bay and fires them

with a luminist's white,
igniting everything white,
and, as suddenly,

as the mist changes density,
is defused. The light enters
the afternoon and finds us

at work like this:
one is asleep
in an upstairs room,

another reads in the runway
where the view is only forest,
the more stable landscape

in a storm. She's reading
a story about injustice
and the right to extremes,

of something uncomplicated
like a pair of horses starved
by angry men, the death of the hero,

and the darkening the author sensed
in 19th-century Europe.
So she's reading on a cane couch,

her friend is preparing the evening meal,
and I'm on my way out of the house
to walk awhile in the afternoon,

or what's left of it.
We've lost something here:
a day of perfect light,

a little time in the sun
with the birds
at work, carrying out

their natural chores,
the flock of sails adrift
at another end of the bay.

But I'm not thinking of sunlight,
or the sailing boats,
or the horses of Michael Kohlhaas.

I could lie down
with my sleeping friend
and hold her as the storm

terrorizes the landscape,
sleep awhile next to her
and wake in the night

with the sound of rain
barely audible, tapping
the walls of the house.

I remain outside
in the rain and the darkening,
and look back at the house

where those close to me
are at work,
whatever it is.

The white, heavy column
of smoke rises
into the mist, and below,

at the smoke base, the fire
gives to them its necessary heat.
I'll stay here a little longer

and return after dark, to share
the evening meal, the fire,
the small-talk, our right to all this.

Part Three

To a Friend Shot on a Mexican Bus

He's one of the hard talkers,
hitchhiker, runner,
cold-water swimmer.
He walks Broadway
after the bars have closed,
whistling at those willing
to commit harm,
can ignore the tremendous
rush of leftover fish
in the street-trash
of oriental restaurants.
He has fought the wars
he could have
and writes letters of length
that break down upon themselves.
If we talk about him
over a few drinks
we remember the cadence
of his walk,
the arguments he had
with each of us.
He's the one who lost an eye
looking for the club of a pre-bop jazzman
in a forties Kansas City
back street off Troost Avenue,
the friend who called at no-man's hour
to say he needed a friendly voice.
He's the man on the Mexican bus
shot for insulting the dust.
Where were the women
to take him in at night,
the family—
where are we,

the days so entangled these many years
later?
Haven't we
understood this far?
We've hung back,
which was the right thing to do.
We won't insult the dust and die,
we won't die
during the moments
we believe ourselves
beyond the cycles of nature.
We won't die insulting the dust.

LOCAL

They had the power of walking,
their fine, unresolved bodies
mysteries of experience.
In their wake hung the scents

of perfume they wore, like trolling
objects let out from handsome boats.
They seemed then beyond anything local
because it was impossible to know them.

They bought their clothes in Europe
during the summers when English
was something rarely in their mouths—
they brought back accents

and wardrobes to try out
on the depleted local August air
with a little more dissatisfaction
than the year before as they huddled

on weekends, exchanged a little
foreign gossip, and walked to rhythms
in no way local. They were just
exotic: the cut of their hair

as it changed year by year,
the changing gait of their walk
in the mildly autumnal crispness
of their place of internment.

Twenty years later they are no different,
just living through it like us all, holding off
the collapse of the body's biology,
local, regardless of who or where they've been.

30TH

Above Fifth I catch the last
detail of light, a bright wire
over the Hudson, and to the east
the night takes good hold

and settles in. Dark is
the last moment before winter light
throws the switch turning on
the streetlamps along 30th:

called the hour of crime
at Midtown South,
the hour of women in modified clothing
who appear on the four corners

of Madison. The big cars
start their long smooth crawl,
Park to Fifth and back,
the offices empty, and the move

for the rivers begins.
The traffic dies, the streets empty
and set their alarms. This is the flower
district, the fur, the purlieu

of the garment district:
no-man's-land at sundown. Ten years ago
neighbors walked these streets
with the residents of nearby hotels

and wandering couples
from upper Fifth on their way
to Washington Square for park music.
By eleven it would be time to walk

to Peerless Pauline's,
where Jimmy sat at his jazz piano
playing only those songs you could name—
and there were no songs he didn't know,

hammering Pauline's keys, by then
the color of old teeth. Downtown money
brought him to 30th from Harlem,
his first sixty-five years spent on 125th and Lenox—

he'd been at Pauline's for ten.
It was an odd crowd that gathered there:
chauffeurs, bookies, secretaries and supers,
neighbors drawn to local music,

a little talk and beer
before starting back to take on
the burdens of salary. Jimmy died in '80
and Pauline closed the bar,

which ended
my connection to an earlier city,
my own first history with the city—
the end of one thing,

the beginning of something else.
There was talk of upgrading our street,
so many of us stayed on. The uptown prostitutes
shared the same source

and floated down
from 42nd and Times Square like angels
to share our developing neighborhood and catch
the spill-off from the Garden

and the all-night trade
of the 24-hour Korean markets on Madison
and Fifth. The landmark hotels are welfare now
and the new neighborhood drinking spot

is the vestibule
of whatever building some new resident
of 30th has left open, the hours
of business extended to sunrise,

when the sun off the East River
still fires the same intensity of light—
summer or winter—to accompany
the street machinery of 6 A.M.

that pries up another day.
The hard city-light of winter cocks a fist
and those of us who have chosen this ring move
forward, to begin again.

What's not a trade-off?
Facing north I feel the material of jumpsuits
and shirts of garment district designers slipped
over the fabulous mannequins whose presence

is half of every sale.
In the morning light I look down Fifth
and see the bow of the Flatiron to the south,
ready to slip its moorings.

Bon voyage. Bon voyage I call out,
joining the street-talkers' chorus. Along Sixth
I can smell the spectral arrangements,
flowers blossoming out of the night.

Hotel Carlton, Tangier: The Old City

There's a fine rain that finds its way through the screens
of the Carlton.
I'm sitting behind the gauze curtains listening to the street life
of the Socco Chico,
the clinked handful of glasses used for mint tea and juice
in the Café Central.
Down the hall painted a red enamel just short of cheap nail polish
there's a young woman who has a boyfriend from the medina,
and sometimes she calls out
from an afternoon sleep to the Midwest, where her parents listen
for her;
she calls out in distinct American for the green slacks
of her father's friends,
the floral pastels of her mother's friends.
Down the hall a young male traveler calls out from the knot
of initiation dysentery.
Down the hall a group of tenured residents listen quietly
to the rain and Egyptian radio music
sprung from shop stereos in the scented air of freshly cut *kif.*
The rain thickens. I get up and close the window. The air fills
with twenty years
of the marginal transient renters of this room, drifts
from the walls, the painted floorboards,
the curtains, pipes, and tiles of the bathroom, the mattress
floating on a trapezoid of springs.
Through the walls, through the glass of the windows,
I can smell the afternoon meat as it's placed on braziers
protected by straw mats from the rain.
I can smell the pinch of cumin placed on each quickly chopped cube
of meat: beef, chicken,
mutton, and dog. Horse, camel, and cat. And for the hungry,
a sprinkling of rain.

3 A.M. / The Rain

You hear them at night over the dogs,
up from the valley near the sea,

first clear and sharp, then muted,
then alive again as they turn

with the instruments in their hands
to face the directions as they play.

If you choose, you can join the faithful
at that hour, who have come to trade

the small-talk of the day, the evening
soup spun with eggs and lifted

with native bread. The rain
is dripping from the lowered awnings

when you arrive in the square.
The men are occupied at their tables

and hardly notice you fall
into the placement of figures

seated with the light of carbide
lamps repeating down the wet street.

But if you stay in your room when you wake,
if you go to the window to hear the men

with greater clarity, to feel the wind
ride in off the rain and sense the dogs

stationed along the valley roads,
the night remains with you—

the simplicity of it, the rain and rotating
sound of the men releasing their music,

your small part of it all, the way you placed
yourself in the room so that when you return

to this, you see the young man listening
through the rain over the dogs, his back to you.

Dark Night

The moon was wrapped in a cloud,
all the shapes of the Old Mountain faded
    into one shape, and the wind blew down
    from the pine forests of Sidi Amar, up from the Dradeb
    where the shutters were closed against nothing.

The villa was on the Old Mountain, rue Vasco da Gama.
I could hear the trail horses in their stables whinnying softly,
    a confused hen too eager for first light.
    I opened the gate and greeted Vasco the watchdog
    and Larbi, the night watchman. I unlocked the door

to my room, turned on the light, and pulled back
the bedsheets, uncovering five dark inches
    of black centipede against the white cotton
    of newly laundered sheets. In the distance
    I heard the dog pacing the garden below my room

and Larbi making his final rounds down to the river
and back up through the cane. A donkey's ridiculous
    sawing laugh carried up on the salt wind
    from the Atlantic beaches. I took a hanger from the closet
    and hit the dark stitching in the bed, smashing its symmetry.

The moon must have been released suddenly from its bunting
because my window lit up and I could see
    the profile of the plane trees and Larbi as he retired
    to his cane hut with Vasco. I heard him call to Khaddouj,
    his wife, our maid, in the dark, windowless interior

of his house. The villa's colonial owner later told me
she had placed the centipede in my bed—I was the new tenant,
    carrier of the help's grievances.
    The wind troubled the curtains, now illuminated
    in the new light. I let the hanger go.

The body of the centipede lay broken in the pool of sheets.
The paired legs, detached from the thorax and stunned,
    suddenly began to move, run in all the directions
    of the room. I stood back as the moon took position
    over the canebrake. The bestiary of this climate

all at once, and each in its own way, called out—
the hen at nothing at all, the chuckling donkey
    and dreaming dog, the horses
    in their narrow stalls—as the jointed legs of the centipede
    deserted the husk of the body central,

everything of importance removed on reflex, transported
off sleep's white surface. Did I slip into the chair
    in the corner, out of the way, to untie the laces
    of my shoes? It was a night of fitful sleep,
    under the burdened light of the cold Mediterranean moon.

Preparations for the End of the Evening

The light is Spanish on the Moroccan back streets,
late winter, the air begins to hold a little
of the lemon vegetation, the sound of dogs
and flutes carries up the valley, late afternoon.

It is cold enough to continue burning wood
and stay inside. Above, the clouds
promise an early evening, inflated on light,
full, but not ready to come the distance forward.

Although uninvited, I know they have begun
the preparations for the evening meal upstairs;
their cooking finds its way here to remind me
of my own meal, still uncut on the counter.

The watered plants use up the day's fluid
and darken on the terrace; the caged birds there
have shut down for the night, the pets
of a boy here. These nights can be spent

in the custodial care of the fire, the out-of-print
novel, and a little pacing between front door
and back window, where I watch the streetlamps
snap on, listen to the frogs starting up

in the riverbed, where they say a beautiful woman lives
to seduce unwary men. She has the feet of a goat
and those who look into her eyes go crazy—
this being part of the local mythology. Late winter,

and blowing from the east the *levante,*
a wind that pursues the restless population.
The palms appear to change color at night in this season;
the visual rearrangements in the street alarm those

foreign to this place. Who *is* waiting for you there?
Under the streetlamps the little stages
await their players. The sound of dishes upstairs,
the house lights of the valley going out,

the metal shutters slamming shut—
preparations for the end of the evening.
The fire here will always need another stick of wood,
the pot another cut of meat, another sliced vegetable.

The light from the fire plays on the neutral.
At this hour there is no sound that can be identified,
there is nothing in the river except stones and sand
over which the opaque water continues.

The Lesson

Where have they gone?
she asked her father.

To the orchards,
he replied,
where the apples hang
until they can't wait
any longer.

To the shade trees in town,
he said,
where the citizens are distracted
from their daily work
by the musical, repetitious
pill-will-willet
and rapidly repeated
kip-kip-kip
before the tree birds take flight.

To the large scattered trees
where only space abides
and the blown current
of air in open places.

The child is on a softening redwood
watching her father,
listening to the *thwack* of his ax
against the heartwood,
the furred vibration
of the cat's throat in her lap
and the good muted thudding
again and again at her breast.

Part Four

PASTICHE

The cast in this endless contemporary novel,
which attempts to call back a few members
of last century's most polite and youthful
society, will contain two women not quite thirty,
one dark, one fair; their colors (their casts,
it might be written) reflect what can be demonstrated

of their inner selves; and what cannot be
merely witnessed moves to the reader by way
of the writer's detached irony, philosophic
musings, inexact gesture, belonging to
the reader's understanding of how the body works
in its gestures toward others or in solitude.

The young women move in an obstructing light
that can only be 19th-century, so faded, so dusty,
the air so reasonably rehearsed in an appropriate room
of the house. The men are ready to enter
with their carefully selected and described attire.
We have already seen the taller of them

through his bright days at university—
it is Oxford—his actions during the incident
that occurred one hot afternoon while punting
on the river, the falling into bed with the woman
destined to marry the man he will meet
later in the novel, years after this takes place.

What I await are those passages that bring out
the true nature of events,
that clarify what is always almost conscious,
and the pages preceding the love scenes, complicated
and thick with dialogue and internal asides.
But I am losing the thread of narrative. The women and men

are over sherry in that room of the house where
the intensities are to take place. Is Sarah
the name of the fairer of the two women?
And the darker, hers is the more unusual name—
at the moment of the novel the most memorable;
later, the first to be forgotten as the plot fades

into our own events. The room is proportioned
by light coming through the various surfaces
of elaborately complicated glass.
The odor in the room is of roses gone past full bloom,
past the expected red toward reddish-brown,
rimmed with something darker, cartilaginous.

It seems we grow in our anticipation.
We don't ask to whom our destinies are responsible.
I arrive at this moment as they too arrive.
I take her hand in mine and kiss her cheek,
a gesture that acknowledges my restraint
and willingness to continue as we have—

how easy it is to relinquish one context
for another. Her husband's hand is cool and thin,
a little damp. Sarah is introduced to me,
and as the evening progresses I will devote
much of my energy to her, who has already
come to understand the construction of the evening.

There is nothing that isn't poised and ready
for these carefully groomed characters, who
begin to move toward the end of their fiction
in which love and all that's right will come
to no good end—in which love and all that's right
will find the correct ending to their story.

The Death of Li Po

It is reported that the poet Li Po fell out of a boat and was drowned when he tried to embrace the moon's reflection on the water.

Not even their master calligraphers
had a configuration for gesture
that deep, no combination of a master's strokes
could have anticipated his disappearance,
it wasn't in the language.

The hour he pushed away from the shore is uncertain—
his boat light, riding high in the water
and colored indecorously,
nearly celebratory in its pursuit of restraint.

The dark, irregular pattern of current
on the water took him out
to one of the windless centers of the river.

The boat, stilled, turned
on the unseen guiding current
under the pure intensity of moon.

He motioned through his fingers,
beyond now the swirling eddies,
the paired butterflies and various mosses.

He removed his colorless robe
that had nothing of the impure to violate
the water's white abstraction.

The moonlight that was everywhere
reflected around the circumference of his arms,
which he spread to embrace the white surrogate
imprinted thinly on the skin of water
as he passed through that perfect circle of light.

At Dante's Tomb

Too austere even for Dante

this place of interment
   at seaside Ravenna.
      The cold, polished wall

fixes something deathly here,
   but of stone not flesh.
      Nothing of the fecund earth

holding Shelley and Keats,
   their good friend Severn,
      Hardy's singers of that shadowy wall

and history-haunted street.
   Inscription. Gold flake and black marble.
      This little formal room,

the purple ghost of Dante
   for those not superstitious
      that hovers here

among the four worlds we inhabit.

CARAVAGGIO

Men like to see a familiar face.
They like to recognize a particular claret
    at the house of a friend during dinner
    or the composition of a certain painter.

They like to know a woman in a crowd,
to exchange a few words and move on.
    It is the familiar that moves them,
    but only that vague feeling of recognition—

not habit but déjà vu, nothing steady—something
just recognizable: a construction or landscape
    that brings back part of their past,
    that in a moment is relived and released.

Men like to recognize each other
where they find a little of themselves;
    they like to be recognized and approached.
    They stand before the mirror as they imagine

they stand before the world, a posture
exactly situated, the expression one of
    slightly bemused recognition. I am standing
    in one of the cold museums of Rome;

it is the end of the 16th century on the canvas
that dominates the room of the Galleria Nazionale
    as the reflected face of young Narcissus
    dominates Narcissus rendered

by the bandit Caravaggio, dead at thirty-seven of malaria
on his way back to Rome. An artist and murderer—
    and the master of light and composition.
    It is the light of recognition in each canvas

that men look into as they stand
before his work—what they recognize
    in themselves, of where they are,
    no matter who or where they happen to be.

Below Keats's Room, First Light

I won't forget
standing at the foot of that long marble stair
watching the window where Severn, in silhouette,
tossed the meal Keats rejected—perhaps his last fair

act of criticism as he lay damp
and longing for Fanny Brawne's face,
his young black lungs filling, the light of the lamp
aglow in his room. No one was in that place,

the square had only the fountain sound, some mist,
and no trace of the unacceptable meal. *Toss it*
Keats called weakly to the friend he already missed.
In the Piazza di Spagna, at that hour, I heard Keats say it.

after Wilbur

Pound

It was a night one might have expected
of Venice:
mid-December, mid-Sixties,
a vaporetto
heading for Accademia—
I was looking for a cheap meal.
It hadn't stopped raining all week
and it was cold,
the dampness above the water
about the same as in,
although there was a little human warmth
in the cabin
where I sat watching the landings
interrupted by the ancient villas
float past the fogged windows—
ghostly, routine, and cold.
It seemed to me, at twenty, like the 19th century,
and I must have written as much
on the pad I kept
in my army surplus jacket.
The light, the sense of history
at night in winter
when time takes on mobility,
the weather rough, unamiable,
made the ride uncomfortable but important.
An old man next to me
watched as I tried to elaborate
the experience. Placing my hand
over the words of my descriptive prose
set out in obsessive syllabics,
I looked over at him.
It was Gaudier-Brzeska's portrait of Pound
that prefaces *Personae*
with the eyes colored in,

steady and there.
Not knowing what to say I asked him
what came to mind. I asked him
if he spoke English.
The eyes, blue, humorous and bored,
looked at me a moment.
Nope, he said
in perfect American,
keeping it simple.

House in Damariscotta

Imperfection is the language of art . . .

—ROBERT LOWELL

If it hadn't been for the Kavanaughs'
yellow mansion on the hill,
we wouldn't have found
your little gray-and-white Cape
across the meadow, down from the graveyard

where the Kavanaugh family is buried.
The house is still there
although the red splash of Indian maize
has been taken away.

On that hot afternoon by the mills,
which have been turned into a garage,
it was hard to imagine the snowplow,
its red and blue lights

and the casting off of snow.
But driving by your house on its hill
it was possible to imagine
the two of you,
simmering like wasps

behind the now-remodeled walls.
It was summer and we felt like Maine's
most recent acquisitions.
We have our own house an hour away,
on a bay where the tides

move up and down the beach
a hundred feet.
It's not rugged
but it is good looking,
with only the Bailey Island bridge

between us and open sea.
We drove to Damariscotta
to find the house
in which you spent
that snow-bound winter,

where you kept a list of birds—
you and your old flame.
But we couldn't go in.
Instead we drove back up the hill

to the stand of pines to watch
the family of eagles
with a German couple
and their pair of Zeiss binoculars.
The male stayed near the nest,

which looked like the bread basket
for the town of Damariscotta.
The female was in flight
and even high in the air
she was spectacular,

tremendous in size and graceful,
her merciless eye perusing
the land that circled out
from the base of her home-wood—
that nest fixed there, suspended.

Nightwork

The humid night has thrown
against its dark wall
a fistful of fireflies

that snap on and die,
are born again elsewhere
in the line of small trees

growing off the slopes
over Harpswell Bay.
They are fishing for herring

with nets that enclose
this part of the bay.
The sounds of the fishermen

are close—they are setting out
their nets, the engines
starting up, turning off,

the voiced interrogative *Bill?*
I awaken in the dark
not from dream or the stopped,

heavy night, but to their work,
their sounds of such clarity
they could be in this room—

as if they are not on the water at all,
but part of my sleeplessness,
like a radio left on during a night

of fitful sleep, or the presence
of a passing but important intimacy
that makes constant sleep so difficult.

. . .

Out in the yard at three,
partly asleep
during the lunar eclipse,

I watch the stationed boats and trees
go out a shade at a time
under the pinched wafer.

The colorless day lilies
collapse around me,
their scent growing keener

under the darkened nickel,
hole-in-the-sky,
one-eye rolled up for once,

and only the backup summer
constellations to provide
the muted light above me.

. . .

Now to wake into the morning,
the body of bay stitched
with herring nets,

herons at water's edge,
the house a cupboard
of damp wood holding

a few earthly treasures.
Here in this room
there's a bay

on which I've slept out
another story to find myself
askew in the wash

of early light,
the water again ironed
under a gull's flight.

An armada of peaceful boats
slides on a line
into the channel beyond

the far point,
the sails a unified color
of white light.

. . .

There is an island not far from the point
where the mainland gives out.
A woman lives there,

on the leeward side,
her well up a path feet deep
with the deciduous spoilage

of the island trees
and nothing else
but the layered rocks

studded with black quartz
that abut the ocean,
the thousand gulls,

and two fish hawks
that nest in the tree
above the well.

Outside her glassed-in kitchen
there is a great deal
of weather to consider,

the attending light,
the wildlife
active on the water surface.

At sundown the insects rise
to irritate the air
and our participation

in the sensible passing
into night. We start
the fire and evening meal.

It is what we say now—
the water breaking down
outside, the body of island

endlessly dark—that gets taken
back to the mainland. Tonight
we share the hundred true things.

• • •

One day I'll give up this piece of land
over the water, backed by pines
and minor fields,

bullied by the sand and salt wind.
And once gone,
there'll be no need

to return to the fish spine
and bay rock, to the skittish
lobster that scuttles

beneath the Whaler
and later lends its shell
to the sea brine, the coastal

wash-up, the tidal scar
that's momentary but recurring.
Perhaps years from now, and miles,

it will be possible to recall
this land, the dark subjugating
nights attached to the coast here.

. . .

Farther north I had a friend
who sat in a chair by the window
thinking over his own geography:

the refined English lawn,
the surf on his serrated rock-beach,
and the island, barely visible, beyond,

matte on the reflecting skin of summer bay.
Each evening he knew that on another
he would approach the island

and emerge from the water
unalterably changed, indifferent
to his piece of land on the north coast.

. . .

Leaving is what I take up in the evening.
By morning I have found a way
to stay on another day. The herons

follow the tide up the beach and fly off,
the tide slips back, I take stock.
By evening it is time to leave again.

My friend up the coast
disappeared one night
after a dinner with some people he knew.

They found him a few days later
on his own beach, at the tide mark.
There's not much left but the attempt to stay.

• • •

I want to protect the day lilies
from the direct light of the sun,
from the storms that flare up

off a calm sea with so little warning
that the summer people are still sunning
when the first unexpected rush of wind

brings on the curtain of rain.
I want the nights to myself,
with no other lamp than my own

illuminating the pages as I turn them,
as the rain turns the still-green
shingles of my house to wine.

I want the memory of this land
in the air when there is only
forest, or flatland, or mountain.

I want this encrusting air to roughen
the surfaces of wherever I find myself,
so when the lights go out up inland roads

there will be again the saline smell of tidal deposits,
the appeased gull-cry calling out,
the ongoing sea-sound in the shell of night.

Part Five

The Summer Rentals

for my father

Today we went to see the summer rentals
that belong to Mrs. Marian Forster.
Her house, up the road from the Camden marina,
was off to the left, placed on the bay
across from the Curtis Island lighthouse.

She was a talker, with a quick, momentary smile—
you would have likened it to a jab,
but would have liked her handsome good looks.
I thought of you because she had just married
a man she knew in Los Angeles thirty years ago

who was built like you, tall and thin, elegant
in his dark suit and tie. A European with your face,
had you lived long enough, and your good humor
that lived in the eyes. His name was Harry.
Over proper drinks we talked summer rentals

with Mrs. Forster, or Mrs. Someone Else now—
we weren't given Harry's last name.
It was clear from the way he watched her
he was in love for the first time,
or still in love with his first love.

Talking to him was like talking to you.
Although I don't think we spoke of anything
in particular, it was like the talk we had
tossing a ball back and forth outside our house,
or walking down Van Nuys Boulevard.

Mrs. Forster liked us—we were "an interesting couple."
She took Jeanne's face in her hands
and asked me, "Is this a summer thing?"
Mrs. Forster, working the world of possibility,
never lost the spirit of romance.

She showed us, with delicate speed, "the small house,"
in which we could hear the sounds of the bay—
but not as well as in her house, she explained.
The stove in our kitchen had only four burners
and used electric heat, on which she refused to cook,

hers being a Garland with six gas burners
and a salamander, suitable for her style of living.
She told us the guests who lived on her property
had keys to every door, but as we grew silent,
followed with a confirmation that she of all people

believed in the importance of privacy.
I wonder what you would have thought.
Certainly you would have voted against renting,
in spite of being charmed by Mrs. Forster
and her property's flawless situation on the water.

We returned to her house and the women wandered off
to look at other rooms, pieces of furniture,
photographs of the second wedding and of her first husband,
who seemed someone rarely referred to in that house.
Harry and I talked a bit about his work in California,

his new life with Mrs. Forster, and he even explained
that when Mr. Forster died he had arrived to take her
"out of the woods." I knew he was Swedish
by the quick intake of breath that occurred when I said
something he agreed with. His sidelong glance and smile

presented the one context we could share.
It seemed to me, as we talked, that he knew
I was talking to you.
It was his eyes that allowed me to imagine asking
the two or three things I've wanted to ask you.

As we left, knowing it would be impossible to return,
I remembered the first room I rented, against your better judgment,
as well as the room where I last saw you. I shook Harry's hand.
It was large and dry and surprisingly strong. As strong,
I returned the handshake you taught me as a boy.

Like Something Out of the Ordinary

Nothing out of the ordinary.
The shrill, terrifying whistles go off at noon.
And then the lulling bells of afternoon,

the scented wind off the bay by evening.
At night, the leaves of the pine trees
absorb the wind, and a stillness arrives

that provokes reverie.
Don't make a fiction out of this.
The dawn spreads up Harpswell Bay

between the spindly legs of a heron,
over the rocks and mussels of low tide,
up the embankment and into the window

where I again await the light. *Greet it!*
you say behind me, sitting up in bed.
You hold the sheet to your breasts,

embarrassed by the energy of two exposures.
Greet it! You've fallen back to sleep.
It might be that coffee will expel my night's dreaming.

It might be there are possibilities in bodies
that haven't settled down. It might be
we take chances moving along the thread of sleep,

serving the attitudes we've left to chance
by such casual living. It might be that this
is the only way we know how to live: *living it!*

Or *greeting it!* Or whatever it is that must be done.
It might be nothing out of the ordinary, but finding the sun
after a night of looking beyond the solace of sleep seems *good,*

no? I'm not making something false out of this.
I don't know where you've gotten to or where we've been.
It must have seemed like *just for the moment,* like something

merely passing, before we came upon the simplicity of *greeting it.*

EPITHALAMIUM

In the streets the crowds go about their business
like they always do here, in the rain, or in the clear
cold mornings before the shops close for the midday.

It is possible to do nothing but participate outside
along with everyone else, to look through the glass
and imagine unwrapping what is perfectly displayed.

They have lit small oil lamps the entire length
of the Via di Ripetta, where our rooms are ready for you.
The only information you need now is to know

that the walls are salmon-colored and there are carpets
to make the mornings easier to negotiate. The kitchen
is serviceable—enough for coffee and good toast.

We'll walk through the city that is so familiar to us:
the Caravaggios in San Luigi and the Piazza del Popolo,
and the *trattorie* sprinkled like *parmigiano* over the city.

I have alerted the notaries and the witnesses,
the officials at the Campidoglio and the embassy,
and the offices that will ask if there is anything

that speaks against what we're about to do. Even
the gold bands have been located in Via della Croce—
the time has come. I am waiting for you.

Rome
December, 1982

Naming the Unborn

Marry late and the next question
concerns children.

Who doesn't want a child
before they are taken away?

Of a sleepless night
I've imagined a girl,

myself a devoted but strict,
adoring father.

To call her by name now
could be bad luck,

although my superstitions
are easily overcome:

a piece of paper
in the absence of wood. I call her

by her hundred names,
touch wood,

and await what will come,
this vigil we keep for the nameless.

Walking in the 15th Century

There are angels on the road from San Sepulcro
to Monterchi, and olive trees;
there are grapevines that bring forth
the Umbrian wine Piero drinks
before he goes back
to his pregnant Madonna and the women
attending her. She too will travel this road,
but long after we've gone.

The 15th-century sun is up and to us
it seems *youthful*. It seems *uncomplicated.*
There are angels on the road,
or perhaps they remind us of angels
we've seen on the old canvases
five hundred years later. The air
this time of year feels strict,
the leaves, early autumn, fugacious.

Sometimes, if the distance is not too great,
it is possible for the unborn
to walk with us. Perhaps they are the angels.
Piero might have experienced his Madonna's child,
destined through his art to remain
in utero forever, in this way.
My daughter and I continue along the road;
the wind travels with us.

Piero will have to hurry along to catch us
before we reach the spectral hill town
and the little chapel a kilometer beyond it
that awaits his Madonna.
She must be there when I arrive
with the mother of our unborn child
to pay the caretaker the few hundred lire
for a look.

Child Running

The little girl runs too quickly in the summer afternoon.
It is late afternoon and she runs along the beach,
  her parents nowhere in sight, no relatives, only
  the waves of the bay repeating alongside her

as she runs the hysterical, off-balance run of children
overly excited, anticipating, dramatic, out of control.
  It might be the small red boat at the end of the bay,
  or the heron following back the tide after herring,

or the group of children playing farther down the beach
with a ball. Something calls to her. As far as
  I'm concerned, there are too many boats alight in the bay,
  too many flying insects. I'm thinking of Marianne Moore's monkeys,

who winked too much, as I stand at night on this lawn looking at the lights
across the water, of her elephants with fog-colored skin
  during the overcast mornings here, of the day's events,
  the tidal movement on the beach, the weather and menus for tomorrow.

Every day there is one less day no matter what you believe,
or in whom. This, of course, discounting the afterlife.
  If you think too much about what there is
  you begin to lose what you have.

This is foreshadowing and it preoccupies me. In my hand
a piece of burnt toast, a grown woman asleep where I left her,
  her body curled around the shape I no longer inhabit.
  On loan, the makeup of what is visible at this hour.

The playing child is one distraction, the warmth of the day
another. The layout of the scene below demands attention—
  it is not a matter of description but of focus. The weather's
  holding. What's one ecstatic child running on the beach?

Words of Advice

Language held you above the water,
you breathed,
you took hold of yourself.
Off the millponds, light
fired the discursive
opportunities of the scene.
You called back
pre-dark dinners as a child
among those of your blood.
Write me
someone with years of stability
asked of you
as another year turned.
And what was it your mother told you
never to forget?
They've taken away your father
and the little song
you remember him by.
It goes like this. . . .

You called back the young women—
their slender, lonely bodies
stayed awhile at your side,
they said what they had to.
Make it easy on yourself;
there comes a time
when you'll sit down alone,
finished with yet another story,
and begin to assemble
what has been given over to you—
your face remembers
its repertoire of moves
and there is a song
that keeps you awake.

A single detail of light
is dragged over the water.
You called back
something you were told
not long before your father's death.
It was a little kindly advice,
surviving on the body of its melody,
the lyrics long ago lost on you.

The Afternoon: Mid-December

1.

There was a woman
who learned languages

as a child of missionaries,
who read me

stories she translated
from the Japanese

before I slept,
the fire in our family house

still aglow. Years from there,
sitting on a bench

in the afternoon air,
I drift a little in time

and hear her voice speaking stories
over the popping of the greenwood fire,

calling back a little
of that fictional atmosphere,

the ubiquitous sanatorium
high in the mountains, a long trip

by train for visitors, and
a tubercular protagonist who

waits for his friend to arrive,
their relationship never disclosed.

He watches from a chair in the yard,
or from his bed, the stripes

of the afternoon sun forking in,
a centipede visible on the fence

outside his window, the wind
riffling the available vegetation.

The patient does not recover
and the visitor, if she arrives at all,

is sullen but delicately beautiful,
uncommunicative but wildly perceptive.

2.

I must have thought she spoke to me
as I sat in the square reading

from someone's uniform edition.
She was only talking to a friend.

Two plain women who spoke of something
ordinary. It is the imagined and half-heard

conversation that survives and is repeated
when alone.

I must have thought she spoke to me,
that she touched my arm.

I looked up and the light
was English, there were children

in the park with packages
and scarved women in black coats

moving quickly before the coming dark.
There were a few muddied flyers

on the snow, something about
no one being alone.

I must have thought she spoke to me.
She touched my arm and I looked up.

3.

If I anticipate the end of the year
I recall the brief, bitter nights

of mounting festivities throughout the city,
the windows building the spectacle

as we passed them. The winter had each of us
wrapped as if for someone else,

and everyone moved with a kindlier
momentum and truer certainty.

My family is everywhere now.
How would our father

have gathered us together
for the days of celebration?

Amaryllis

Far out beyond the forest I could hear
the calling of loud progress . . .

—EDWIN ARLINGTON ROBINSON

Through the city the flocks are led
to their last standing, and we look to John,
not Luke, to understand the other life.
Our lessons begin with what is less beautiful.

As I knelt by the grave of our mother
a storm passed over us, and a harsh rain
snapped the necks of the long-stemmed tuberoses
we brought to honor memory. The rain

passed and left the day without a breeze,
left the humid heat that follows summer rain.
One by one those attending the dead
filed through the mud of the cemetery

until I was left alone, standing there
in the place of stillness. And soon the light
began to fade and there was only
the loneliness of the afterlife that hung

just beyond the sickening scent of unrooted
flowers tightening on their last day.
Around so many dead the ante is one
more indispensable member of the living—

we are to imagine that person here on another day
and to understand how the women and men
who lie here have each been the imagined.
As I stood by this graveside, giving over

one of the beloved to the sanctified earth,
a man I hadn't seen touched my arm
and motioned for me to follow him.
Distraught, as he must have been each time here,

he brought me to the one unflowered grave
and placed my hand on the stone with his
wife's name cut into it. And then he dropped
to his knees in the mud and began to rock.

There must have been a brief song to accompany
the palsied hand and opaque eye,
but I heard only the whine of tires
pursuing the expressway,

the water dropping through the trees. I watched him there
as he rocked in the mud and spoke to her without a sound—
with witness he appeared no longer lonely under this
seasonable summer weather. I touched

his little shoulder and he stood up.
His loss meant nothing to me—and mine
nothing to him, not this loss or my losses to come,
not yet finished with the landscape enclosed here.

I remember thinking the man too old
to stand so long like this. He brought no flowers,
hadn't dressed up, didn't know what to say
as we stood there, the knees of his pants

baggy with mud. He hadn't said a word,
but it was his loss that seemed at that moment
the one attended to. Small birds
clouded the air, the hum of evening traffic grew.